The Demon Bike Rider

There was a ghost on Barker's Bonk: a horned demon that made a terrible howling noise as it glided along in the dusk – on a bicycle. When Mike and his friends first heard about the Demon Bike Rider they thought a bike-riding ghost could only be a joke. But then one night they saw the DBR – and heard it – and suddenly they were running so fast there was no time to laugh.

They had to discover who – or what – the DBR was, but other odd things kept happening. A mysterious stranger appeared to be making secret explorations of the old cottage on the Bonk. And who on earth planted a whole lot of trees upside down in Mr Whitehurst's garden?

It was all to do with the Demon Bike Rider, whose story was finally unravelled with as much hilarity as haunting.

The Demon Bike Rider

ROBERT LEESON

Illustrated by Jim Russell

Young Lions

First published 1976 by William Collins Sons & Co. Ltd
First published in Young Lions 1977
Ninth impression March 1989

Young Lions is an imprint of
the Children's Division, part of
the Collins Publishing Group,
8 Grafton Street, London W1X 3LA

Printed and bound in Great Britain by
William Collins Sons & Co. Ltd, Glasgow

Contents

For Alison

Hitinkati shan efasee
Ha pohem lof liazadree

DEMON BIKE RIDER'S SONG

I

A Ghost
on Barker's Bonk

Ghosts are supposed to come in winter, when it's dark and spooky. But this one came in summer – in the middle of a heat wave.

I heard about it one evening just after we'd started the holidays. I was sitting by the kitchen window having my tea. The programme I was watching had just finished, so I leaned across the table to switch off, when Dad came in by the back door.

'Don't switch the telly off, Mike,' he said.

'Too late, lad. Magic Roundabout's finished,' said Mum.

'Very funny,' he answered. 'As it happens, I want the weather forecast.' He took his cap off and wiped his forehead. The cap made a red ring round over his eyebrows.

The weather forecast came on, half-way through. '... rain will spread northwards during the night...' Dad looked out of the window. The sky was bright blue and pink over the moors.

'Rain will spread ... who are they trying to kid? I tell you, that forecast has never been the same since they had women doing it.'

'That'll be enough from you,' said Mum. 'You'll just have to get the hose mended and water the garden.'

'I was thinking of walking down to the club. I'll fix the hose when I get back.'

'I've got a better idea, Tom Baxter. You mend the hose. I'll finish up here and then we'll both go down to the club.'

Dad sighed. 'One of these days I shall win an argument.' He went out into the garden. I slid towards the door.

'Where are you off to, then?'

'Going up the Bonk, Mum.'

'Well, side these dishes first. If you get back before we do, you know where the key is.'

I did. Under a loose brick in the back door step. Why we never got burgled was a miracle. Dad reckoned it wasn't worth trailing up Round Hill to break into our place. We live up the hill from Bugletown. If you look down our road, you can see the council estate further down the hill, then the low level sidings where Dad works, then the railway arches. And, just beyond that, the comprehensive school where I'm going in the autumn.

I ran to the end of our road and turned up the hill, past three more streets like ours and then along Bishop's Road, where the best people in Bugletown live (if you take their word for it). From Bishop's Road you get into the park and once you're across the park, there's open ground with grass and some bushes.

A path winds up to a bank about ten or fifteen feet high, almost like a little cliff in the places where the soil and sand show through. This is Barker's Bonk and at the top there's nothing in front of you – only the moors.

Over on your right, along the Bonk, there's a little white cottage where Mr Walker the woodman lives. I bet it's lonely in winter, but he doesn't seem to mind. Much closer, on the left almost on top of you as you climb up the path, is an old oak tree.

Beyond the oak tree is another old cottage, but not a friendly one like Mr Walker's. It's a creepy place, half ruined, with a wall round the garden. We keep away from there.

Our place is the old oak tree. That's fantastic.

It grows sideways out of the top of the Bonk. I suppose it did stand upright once, but the ground under the roots has been washed away by the rain and the tree leans out into the air. If you climb out on the trunk, it's like walking the plank. You're ten feet up over the path. When you lie down with the leaves all round and close your eyes and listen to the wind, the boughs creak. You can imagine you're on a sailing ship.

When I reached the Bonk, my friends were already there, sitting in the branches. They'd saved me my favourite place about half-way along. Furthest out, right among the smallest branches was Ranji. He had that place because he was the lightest, he said. Really it was because he had the most nerve. My spot was next to his. I could sit on the main trunk with my back to one of the biggest boughs. Then came Sandra and next her kid

brother Andrew. Sandra was thirteen and really too old for us, but she and Andrew had no mother and he needed looking after. So she stuck with us. At least she used to say 'I'm stuck with you lot.'

The kids made up a rhyme about Sandra and Andrew:

'Sandy Andy, Andy Sandy.
'He's as fat as sugar candy.
'She can't run because she's bandy.'

It was true about him. He was plump as a pudding. But she *could* run. In fact they didn't sing that song unless they had half a street start. You don't take liberties with Sandra.

So there we were that evening, sitting and lying among the leaves of the old sideways tree that stuck out from Barker's Bonk. That was where it all started, and it was fat little Andrew that started it.

We were chatting away about nothing special, when he dropped his bombshell.

'Hey, have you heard? They've seen a ghost on the Bonk.'

2

'Who Was Barker?'

'Ghost?' I said. 'Get off, you're joking.'

Andy's face got all red and puffed up. 'I'm not. It's true. Sam Taylor says he's seen it.'

Ranji rose up between the leaves at the end of the tree. 'Spotty Sam is a gigantic liar.'

'If Sam heard you say that, he'd thump you, Ranji.'

'So what? He's still a liar.'

'Shut up, you lot,' said Sandra. 'I want to hear about the ghost. What is it? What does it do? Does it wear a white sheet and rattle chains?'

Andrew ignored these questions.

'It's called the Demon Bike Rider.'

Ranji and I punched one another. 'Demon Bike Rider . . . the only free-wheeling ghost in captivity . . . ghost changes gear . . . ghost loses chain . . .

ghost gets puncture.' We fell about so much we nearly dropped out of the tree.

'You two belt up, or else,' said Sandra.

We did.

Andrew went on. 'The Demon Bike Rider rides at dusk, just after sunset. He rides along the top of the Bonk to the old ruined house. Then he – I mean it – rides back and vanishes by this tree.'

'This tree?' That shook us.

'Yes.'

'What does it look like?' I asked after a moment's silence.

Andrew looked baffled for a minute. 'They didn't really say . . .'

'I bet they didn't stay to find out,' said Ranji.

'Oh, they reckoned it made a horrible noise, though,' said Andrew.

'Like what?'

'Like howling.'

Andrew looked round. He could see he'd shaken us and he was pleased with himself.

Sandra shivered. 'Maybe it's someone playing a joke.'

'On who?' I asked. 'Who comes up Barker's Bonk after dark?'

'Spotty Sam and his girl friend,' said Ranji.

'I know!' said Sandra. 'It must be the ghost of Barker.'

'Who was Barker?' wondered Ranji.

But none of us knew.

'Perhaps,' Sandra tried, 'it's someone who died for love – like Romeo and Juliet.'

'On a bike?'

'You have no soul, Mike Baxter.' Sandra jumped to her feet and scrambled to the ground. 'It's getting dark, we'd better get off home.'

We all began to climb along the tree trunk. Andrew had just reached the roots when he stopped. I could see his face white in the dusk.

'Hey, listen.'

We listened.

'I heard someone call.'

'Don't be daft. You've got ghosts on the brain,' said Sandra.

'He's got no brain,' I said.

'Hey, there it is again.'

We listened. My heart thumped. Someone *was* calling.

Then Sandra laughed.

'It's Mr Walker. He's down there on the road with his handcart. Come on, let's help him push it up to the top.'

We followed her along the Bonk and down the

path. No one wanted to stay at the top any more. We found Mr Walker with the handcart tipped up, resting under the oak tree.

'Shall we give you a push up to the top, Mr Walker?' asked Sandra.

'Thanks, love, that's very kind.' Mr Walker wiped his big red face with his sleeve. 'It's hot work when the old cart's loaded.'

'What have you got in there?' I asked as we helped push the cart up the slope.

'Tackle, saws, axes, hammers, wedges and some young trees.'

'Oh, what sort?'

'Two limes, a rowan, a horse chestnut, a couple of beeches, bits of pieces.'

'What are you doing with them?' asked Andrew.

'Don't you be nosey, our Andrew.' Sandra looked annoyed.

Mr Walker laughed.

'We're at the top now, kids. Thanks a lot. That was a big help.'

We stood a moment at the top of the slope. We could see the lights of the town below, but the moors were getting darker.

'You know, you ought to be careful up that old oak tree. One of these days you'll fall out.'

'Oh, we'll be all right, Mr Walker.'

'I daresay you will, Sandra. Good night then, kids.' Mr Walker began to push his handcart along the top of the ridge towards his cottage.

'Mr Walker,' Sandra called.

'Yes?'

'Who was Barker?'

Mr Walker stopped. We could just see him in the dusk.

'He was an old fool.'

'Why?'

'Because he chopped all the trees down, round here. He was going to sell the land and make a lot of money. But he died. And you can't use money where he's gone. You get off home now, kids. Good night.'

'Mr Walker!'

'Yes?'

'Did Barker have a bike?'

'Eh?'

'Did Barker have a bike?'

We heard Mr Walker laugh in the darkness.

'Oh ah. He used to ride it up and down on the Bonk, thinking of all the money he was going to make. Silly old fool.'

'Good night, Mr Walker.'

'Good night, kids. Straight home, now.'

We didn't stop running until we were right through the park.

I got home before Mum and Dad came back. The garden hose was lying in the yard. It didn't look mended to me.

3

Ghost-watch

Next day I had to stay in for the morning. Mum was out cleaning offices and she was expecting some plants to arrive for the garden – to keep the hose company I suppose. They never came but I still had to stay in all morning. I knew the other kids had gone swimming, so I was choked.

But when I got to the park, I found the others hadn't been swimming after all. They'd been lying on the grass watching Mr Walker and his mate work on a big fallen tree. They were having trouble with the saw. I lay down on the grass and looked up at the sky. The sun was blazing hot, but there was a cool breeze. I almost went to sleep.

Sandra was talking to Mr Walker.

'Why were you so sarky about Mr Barker last night?'

'How do you mean?'

'You were going on about him chopping down trees. And you and Bill chop trees down.'

There was a minute's silence before Mr Walker answered. He seemed in a bit of a mood.

'Chopping trees down is my job, Sandra. I chop them down when they need it, like this one here, rotten through the middle.'

'Oh, ah, Sandra,' said Bill, 'and we always plant one for every one we take down.'

Ranji said, 'That was why you had those little trees on your cart last night, wasn't it, Mr Walker?'

'That's right, Ranji.'

'But where do you plant them?'

'Oh, here and there. In the park. Or I give them to people to put in the garden.'

'Or sometimes he pops one in the odd corner, when nobody's looking,' said Bill.

'That'll do. Don't give away trade secrets, Bill.' Mr Walker seemed in a good humour again. Everything was quiet for a while until Andy spoke.

'Can we help you plant trees sometime, Mr Walker?'

'Maybe, Andy. I'll let you know.'

The saw started up again suddenly, like a jet engine.

'Oh, I can't stand that noise,' said Sandra. 'Come on, let's go over to the swings.'

We struggled up and trailed across the park to the roundabout. Ranji, Andy and I jumped on and Sandra started it off. I could see she had something on her mind. While the roundabout was spinning she asked me:

'Can you stay out late tonight, Mike?'

'How late?'

'A bit after dark.'

'Well I don't know.'

'You could tell your mum and dad you're going to the pictures.'

'I suppose so. But why?'

'Tell you in a minute.'

Andrew interrupted, 'Sandra . . .'

'Oh, be quiet a minute. You know what it's all about.' She turned to Ranji. 'Can you stay out?'

He grinned. 'My father is working nights at the mill. He won't know.'

'But your mum?'

'If I say I'm with you, Sandra, she will not worry.'

The roundabout slowed down. Andrew butted in again. 'Sandra . . . I . . .'

'Oh, stop nagging, Andy.'

Sandra leapt from the roundabout and shoved

with her foot. When we were spinning again, she
jumped back on.

'What's it all about, Sandra?' I asked.

'Supposing tonight was a DBR night.'

'DBR. What's that stand for – Don't Be Rotten?'

'Don't be daft. It stands for Demon Bike Rider.'
I stared at her. 'What's the idea?'

She looked mysterious for a moment, then said:
'The idea is, we hide up by the old oak and watch
out for him.'

'But it's not safe.'

'Get away with you. There's four of us. You're
not scared, are you?'

I was, but I wasn't admitting it.

'How about you, Ranji?'

'I can't wait.' His eyes were gleaming.

'OK,' Sandra punched me lightly on the shoulder.
'Meet at the oak at nine o'clock.'

'Sandra . . . I . . .'

'Oh, what is it, Andrew? You are a nag.'

'Can't you stop this thing? I'm going to be sick.'

My mum is like Ranji's: she trusts Sandra. If only
they knew. When she heard I'd be out with Sandra,
Andy and Ranji, she didn't say a word, except,
'Straight home afterwards, mind you.' I didn't

argue. I just finished my tea, watched an old 'Star Trek' repeat and then round about eight, I sidled out. Mum watched me go.

'What have you got your old jumper on for, lad? You'll melt.'

'In case it's cold coming out of the flicks, Mum.'

She looked surprised but said nothing.

It was only half past eight when I reached the Bonk and climbed the old tree, but the others were already on their perches. Sandra and Andrew were playing noughts and crosses in the back of her diary. Ranji in his anorak sat out at the end of the tree like a lifeboatman looking out to sea.

I climbed up and made myself comfortable. The watch began. After a while Ranji moved.

'It will soon be dark.'

I looked up. He was right. The sun had gone down behind the old house on the Bonk, leaving the sky whitey-grey. In the East the sky over the moors was dark already. My foot went to sleep and I started to shake it.

'Be still, you daft thing,' said Sandra. 'You'll scare the ghost off.'

A little breeze began to whisper in the branches. I was getting colder. I could hear Ranji shiver, but he said nothing. Down below, the street lights came on in Bishop's Road. That made the sky look darker. I began to count seconds to myself. One minute, two minutes, three. When I got to five I lost count. Time drifted past. Andrew began to snuffle and Sandra put her arm round him and calmed him down.

Now I couldn't see the others properly, but could just hear them moving. The silence and the darkness deepened. The town lights twinkled down below, but we had to watch the other way, towards the moors. They looked black and unfriendly.

I cleared my throat. My voice squeaked, 'Shall we give up and go home?'

'Sh,' whispered Sandra, fiercely. 'Listen. Listen to that.'

4

The DBR Appears

We listened. We were frozen with fear. From below us on the Bonk came the weirdest sound, like moaning. It came closer. Someone gripped my arm. I jumped. Ranji sat beside me.

'The ghost is singing.'

He was right. It was a strange sound, like a chant. First it was high, then it was low. I could pick out words but they sounded like nothing on earth, like some language from outer space. A light flashed, grew stronger, came nearer, nearer. Now the sound was almost underneath the tree.

Suddenly Ranji drew back a branch leaving a space, and there it was.

A yellow glow half lit up its face, shadowy and horrible and above the head a shape like antlers stood out, black and branching against the glare.

Half-human, half-animal, it glided along, beneath the tree. For a second that seemed like an hour to me, the eerie moaning filled the air round us. Then it died. The yellow light faded.

I felt myself go dizzy. I'd been so scared I was holding my breath. Now all I wanted was to get down from the tree.

'Quick,' whispered Sandra.

I didn't need telling. I was down the tree after her, with Ranji close behind, jumping down on to the grass. I headed for the path down to the park. But Sandra stopped me.

'Not that way, idiot child. This way.' She pointed along the Bonk to the ruined house.

'There's something there. You saw it, didn't you?' she asked.

'Yes. I saw the ghost. Once was enough.'

'Well. Now we find out what it really is. We follow it to the old cottage – if it's there.'

I shook my head.

'All right,' said Sandra. 'Ranji and I'll go. You stay here with Andy.'

Without a word, the two of them set off. But Andrew started to run after them. He didn't like the idea of staying by the old oak any more than I liked the idea of going to the old cottage.

So I sprinted and caught them up. The old

house was just ahead, like a blacker darkness. But there was no sign of the Bike Rider. He had vanished.

'Let's have a quick look behind the house, in the garden,' said Ranji.

'Look, the door's open at the front. We could nip in and have a look through the back window. If there's nothing out at the back, we'll call it a day – or a night,' said Sandra.

'I don't want to go inside,' snuffled Andrew.

'Oh, give over. Look, tell you what. You stay by the door and hold it open. Then we can all run out if we need to.'

Andy wasn't having that. So we all crowded through the front doorway. Inside was empty and bare. At the back there was a little scullery with a back window.

'That looks out on the garden,' said Sandra.

All excited now, we rushed across the floor, scuffing up rubbish and dust with our shoes. There was an awful smell of damp. Ranji reached the window first.

'Look,' he gasped, 'the ghost.'

Not a dozen yards away from the house, among the bushes, a lamp sent a beam up into the night.

And stretching up in its light stood the giant, black, antlered figure. Now it bent down. Its arms moved like huge wings in the lamp's glare.

'It's taking its horns off,' I whispered.

'Hey, it is, too. Now it's digging,' said Sandra.

'Right. But what for?'

'Somebody's grave,' breathed Ranji.

That was enough for Andrew. He let out a howl and ran for the front door. Sandra leapt after him. In the garden the black figure turned, grabbed the lamp and moved towards the house. Ranji and I both ran for it. He reached the front door two yards ahead of me. As I followed him, I thought I heard someone fumble with the latch of the back door.

I dived through the front doorway, trying to slam the door behind me as I went. But as I sprang, someone, something, caught at the back of my jumper and held me fast. I panicked. I yelled.

'Sandra, Ranji! He's got me! He's got me!'

5

Ranji Disappears

My yells brought Sandra and Ranji running back. They took one look at me.

'You daft hap'orth, Mike,' gasped Sandra. 'You shut the door on your own jumper. It's caught in the jamb – quick!'

She pushed the door open a few inches, Ranji pulled at me and I shot out like a cork from a bottle. In seconds we were charging along the Bonk like the US cavalry late for a Western.

By the oak we slowed down. No one was following.

Suddenly Sandra burst into laughter. 'Help, help, he's got me, he's got me,' she choked.

'Oh belt up,' I snarled.

Ranji slapped me on the back. 'Never mind, Mike, we saved you from a fate worse than death.'

'It's not funny. He was only just behind me,' I gasped.

We reached the path into the park and slowed down to a walk to get our breath back.

'Look, Mike,' said Sandra. 'I don't know who or what the old Demon Bike Rider is, but it can't be a ghost.'

'What makes you so sure?'

'Well, whoever was in the garden must have heard our Andy yowling. He came to see what it was. Right?'

'So?'

'Well, ghosts can't hear, can they? I mean ghosts are like computers. They have a programme. They have to do their haunting bit. They can't change their performance when they get a new idea.'

'All right. So it's not a ghost. So what is it?' I demanded.

Neither of them could think of an answer for that. By now we had walked through the park and I was nearly home anyway. So we said good night and I sneaked into our house. I was in luck. Everyone was out. I was in bed when Mum and Dad arrived, though it was touch and go.

Next day I had to help Mum with the shopping.

33

Then I sloped off to the park. There was no sign of the others. The big tree Mr Walker and Bill had been working on was sawn up and carted off. I wandered up the slope. As I walked I thought about what Sandra and Ranji had said. They reckoned the Demon Bike Rider wasn't a ghost. But if it wasn't a ghost what was it? Who, or what, could be digging in a deserted garden after dark? Who could be singing songs (if you could call it singing) in that grotty voice?

Something bounced on my head. It was an oak apple. I looked up and found myself under the old tree. Ranji was looking down at me, grinning. When I climbed up I found he was on his own. He had been busy thinking, like me. And he'd been writing something down.

'I have tried to remember the words of the song the Demon Rider was singing last night,' he said and handed me a piece of paper.

I read what he had written, slowly. 'Hit-ing-a-dish-a . . .' I thought for a second.

'That's nearly it, Ranji. But I'm sure the last bit went like this.'

I handed him back his paper and now I tried to imitate the sound we'd heard the night before.

Ranji screwed up his face. 'What a terrible noise, Mike.'

34

'Well, the DBR's no Kenneth McKellar.'

He grinned. 'Anyway, I think you're right.' He wrote something. 'See, I've changed the words. Look.'

I looked. Ranji had written this:

'Hitinkati shan efasee
Ha pohem lof liazadree.'

'That's it,' I said. 'But what does it mean, Ranji?'

He shook his head. 'Tell you what, Mike. Let's not go swimming Monday morning. Let's meet the others here early and try to work it all out.'

We stayed in the tree till tea time and then went home. I found our Sis home from her work in the library. Her name's really Laura but she's always been called 'Sis'. I used to think, with her being in the library, she could fiddle me extra books. But she doesn't work in the real library. She's in the reference part behind, where the old blokes read the papers.

She liked the work. She said she was going to be an archivist. I asked her if it was painful, but she ignored that one.

That day she was in a good mood, and so I asked her about the mystery tune. Her eyes went wide as I sang it for her.

'Sounds fantastic,' she said. 'Is it Beethoven's 23rd or "God Save the Queen" backwards? I don't know. Ask me another.'

35

I tried it on Mum, but she said: 'Oh you know I don't like pop songs, Mike.'

So I just had to wait for Monday morning.

I was at the tree early, but the others were there already.

Andrew was dancing up and down with excitement. Sandra waved to me from the top of the Bonk.

'Hey, Mike, hurry up and see what Ranji's found.'

I rushed up to join them. All three were on their knees by the tree-roots. These were huge and stood out from the ground like a giant's knuckles gripping the earth. Between two of the roots was a gap like the entrance to a fox's den. I'd noticed it before, but today it seemed much wider.

'Look down there.'

I looked. At first I could see nothing.

'What's there?'

'There's a spade and some rope at the bottom of that hole.'

'How did it get there?'

'The Demon Bike Rider must have left it. No wonder he seems to vanish when he reaches the tree. He gets off his bike and stows his gear away here.'

'What shall we do?'

'Get it out, that's what.'

'Think we ought?'

'Can't do any harm.'

'How will we get to it?'

'Easy,' smiled Ranji. 'I go down the hole head first. But you hold my ankles so you can pull me back.'

'You'll suffocate down there.'

'Oh no, I can hold my breath under water for hours.'

Sandra held one leg. I held the other. Ranji squirmed down into the hole. His voice sounded muffled.

'I must go in further. I can't quite reach.'

We let him slide further in, till only his feet were showing. Then Andrew said:

'Hey, look out. Here's Mrs Whitehurst coming.'

'Oh no,' said Sandra. He was right though. Mrs Whitehurst, who lived in Bishop's Road and owned about 200 labradors, was taking four of them for a walk. She came up the park path like the *Queen Elizabeth II* behind four tugs. Then she stopped and looked up at the tree, as if she'd heard something.

'Pull him back,' I whispered to Sandra.

We pulled on Ranji's ankles. But as we did, he jerked out of our hands.

Next moment, he'd disappeared.

6

The Indian Rope Trick

For a second Sandra and I gawped like idiots at the hole where Ranji had disappeared. Then we heard a little shriek from Mrs Whitehurst on the path below us. We jumped up and peered over the edge of the Bonk.

There under the tree stood Mrs Whitehurst, her eyes wide open, her arms stretched out, while her labradors pulled four ways at once.

'Look at Ranji,' gasped Sandra.

I looked.

Ranji was dangling in the air upside down. One end of the rope was looped round his ankle, but the other by some chance had caught in the twigs and roots under the tree trunk. Holding a spade in one hand and a stake in the other Ranji was spinning round about a yard from Mrs Whitehurst's nose.

Her eyes got bigger as he swung to and fro.

'Er – who are you, little boy?'

'Ranji Anwas,' he answered politely.

'Could you please stop spinning round like that while I'm talking to you. It's very upsetting.'

'Sorry, Mrs Whitehurst. It is not possible to stop.'

'Quick,' I whispered to Sandra. 'We've got to reach that rope and pull him up. He'll have a rush of blood to the head.'

'You mean she will,' answered Sandra. We clambered out on to the tree trunk and looked around in the branches for the end of the rope.

I heard Mrs Whitehurst say, 'Look – er – Ranji. I know that in your country, people have different customs. I respect them. But in this country we do not . . .'

Sandra found the rope end and we tugged. Ranji jerked suddenly at the other end and swung past Mrs Whitehurst's head. The spade tipped her hat off gently and sent it rolling down the path. Two of the labradors broke loose and rushed off after it. The other two went wild and rushed round her legs, wrapping her up in their leads.

'There's no need to be violent, you know,' she gasped as Ranji swung back for a second time and the stake just missed her left ear.

We heaved again. Ranji rose three feet in the air and dangled over Mrs Whitehurst.

'Sorry. I must go now.' And with these words he went gliding up into the tree.

As he vanished, Mrs Whitehurst gave another little shriek and next minute she was running down the road with the labradors yapping and yowling round her.

We dragged Ranji out to the Bonk and untied the rope. I was amazed that he was actually laughing.

'Oh dear,' he gasped. 'Mrs Whitehurst thinks she has seen the Indian Rope Trick. She'll never get over it.' He rolled over in the grass.

We three dropped down beside him, and tumbled over each other. Ranji got his breath back first.

'Really – it's a bit rude isn't it?'

'What is?'

'Us laughing at Mrs Whitehurst.'

Sandra shrugged. 'Well, she's a bit stuck up – won't do her any harm.'

'He's worse,' I said.

'Who, Ranji?' asked Andy.

'No, you nit. Her husband, Mr Whitehurst, the estate agent.'

'How do you know?'

'My mum cleans his offices. She reckons those

houses he sells are rubbish. She said he'd sell anything with four walls.'

'Hm,' said Ranji, 'he couldn't find anything for my mum and dad.'

'That's different,' said Sandra.

We nodded. It was.

'I'm fed up of staying here,' said Andy.

'You're always fed up of something,' snapped Sandra.

'You're always getting at me.'

'Oh knock it off, you two,' I said.

'It's the heat,' said Ranji. 'This country's terrible.'

We all laughed and felt a bit better.

'Hey,' said Sandra. 'We're daft.'

'Speak for yourself.'

'No, we're sitting here like stewed prunes when there's something smashing to do.'

'Like what?'

She pointed towards the cottage.

'Oh, no,' I said. 'Not Barker's. Not after what we saw there.'

'Come on, Mike. There's no one there now. It's broad daylight. Even Andy's not scared now.'

'Ta very much,' said her brother.

I didn't want to go. But I hadn't really got an excuse. So I got up and we walked slowly along the path. The cottage with its broken down wall looked harmless now. In fact it looked a bit sorry for itself – cracked windows, plaster crumbling between the black beams.

There was a yell from Andy who was running alongside the path. He'd fallen over.

'Pardon me, my daft brother,' Sandra muttered and ran after him. Ranji and I followed. Then I fell.

'That makes two,' said Ranji, and fell over himself. We got up. The grass was long, and underneath were all kinds of lumps and holes.

'There's stones or bricks in the grass.'

Sandra kicked out and made a face. 'Hey, you're right.'

'Tell you something else,' said Ranji. 'They're in a straight line.' He walked forward digging with his heel. 'It stops here, now it goes this way.'

'I know what it is,' I shouted, excited.

'Brainy Mike,' jeered Sandra.

'Give over. It's where a house has been. You know the thing they build it on,' I said.

'Foundations, you mean?' asked Ranji.

'That's right. See, it's in line with Barker's place.'

'Tell you what.' Sandra took charge. 'You two go this way, we'll go that. See if we can find any more.'

We searched for ten minutes, till Andy got

grumpy. Then we walked over and sat on Barker's wall.

'There must have been three cottages there,' said Sandra. 'Two must have been knocked down.'

Ranji nodded: 'I wonder if Barker did it?'

'Perhaps that's why he cut those trees down. He was going to sell it all and make a lot of money. My Dad says you get more money for the land than you do for the buildings. Serves old Barker right,' I said.

'You're talking like Mr Walker,' laughed Sandra.

'Course. If Barker had known Mr Whitehurst, he would have made a bomb.'

'Who, Barker or Mr Whitehurst?' asked Ranji.

'Come on,' said Sandra. 'I'm going inside.' She walked up the garden path and we followed. 'Watch where you go, Andy.'

'He might stumble on something,' said Ranji.

'Oh, very funny,' muttered Andrew.

The old door creaked. Some broken glass crunched as we went into the room.

'OK, Mike and Andy look round down here. Ranji and I'll go upstairs.' Sandra took hold of the old blackened banister.

'Watch those steps, they look rotten,' I called.

'Don't talk daft. Safe as houses.'

While Andy poked around in the fireplace I went

into the little scullery. It had a funny sink, about three inches deep. Imagine cooking, washing and all that in a place like this, I thought. No cooker, no fridge. I looked up. There were no wire ends in the ceiling as there usually are in empty houses. Old Barker didn't even have the electric. I tried the garden door. It was locked.

'That ghost must have had the key,' I called out. Andy didn't answer. There was a creaking noise from the front door. He must have got fed up and gone outside. I looked through the window.

'Hey, look at that,' I called, excited.

The bushes and weeds had been broken down. Somebody had been digging. Whatever had happened last night was real. It wasn't our imagination. But who or what was it?

Sandra and Ranji came clumping down the stairs. I joined them. Andy was still poking about in the chimney bottom.

'Come out of that, Andy. You'll get mucky,' called Sandra.

'I think there's something up here,' he answered.

'I know, half a ton of soot. And soon it'll be all over you.'

Andy went on ferreting.

'Someone was digging in the garden,' I said.

'Ghost or no ghost. Someone's after something round here.'

'Let's go and look,' said Ranji eagerly.

'Back door's locked,' I said.

'Well, let's go out the front way and go round.'

'OK.' Ranji and I rushed, but Sandra was first. She stopped and jerked at the door.

'Hey up. What have you done to the door, Mike Baxter, you daft onk?'

'Me? Nothing. What're you on about?'

Sandra turned to face us. Her face was serious. Andrew stopped his poking in the chimney and asked in a frightened voice: 'What's happened, Sandra?'

She looked grim.

'We're shut in. Somebody's locked the door on us!'

46

7

The Mystery Man

'Locked? It can't be,' I said, suddenly scared. 'We only pushed it to.' Ranji and I both grabbed for the door handle, shaped like a ring, and pulled. It wouldn't budge.

'Oh heck,' sniffed Andy, 'we're trapped.'

'Get off,' snorted his sister. 'We can get out by the window.'

But we couldn't. The window was jammed. Some panes were broken but not enough to get through, even for Andy.

'Hey, wait,' I said. 'I heard that door go a minute or two ago. I thought it was Andy. Someone must have shut it from the outside.'

We looked at one another.

'Let's give a shout, then.'

'Suppose they've locked us up on purpose?'

'Well *they* can let us out on purpose then. *They've* got no right to do that.' Sandra kicked on the door and shouted:

'Hey up, whoever you are, come and let us out.' No one answered. No one came.

'Let's all shout together.' We did. There was a longer silence.

'I know,' said Ranji. 'Let's try the upstairs window.' He and I threw ourselves up the wooden staircase. The upstairs room was low where the rafters sloped down. The window was small and square. It opened with a jerk when we pushed on it. We looked down on to the tangled grass and weeds in front of the house.

'Look,' said Ranji. Coming from the side of the house was a man, big and very smart looking. He was rubbing his hands together as though he'd got dirt on them.

'Hey, mister,' I shouted.

He looked up, his mouth open.

'What the . . .?'

'You locked us in. Can you let us out please?'

'You've no business . . . ah . . .' he shook his head angrily and came towards the door. Ranji and I rushed down the stairs, and as we reached the bottom the key turned in the lock.

The man stood in the doorway looking grim.

'Come out, and quick.'

We shot out on to the path. The man locked the door and put the key in his pocket.

'Now,' he said, looking and sounding unpleasant. 'What do you think you're doing here?'

'Looking for a ghost,' said Andy before Sandra could shut him up.

'A what? Pilfering more like.'

Sandra was angry. 'We never. There's nothing here worth pinching anyway.'

'No – so what are you doing round here then? And what have you been rooting round in the garden for?'

'That wasn't us. That was the Demon Bike Rider.'

'Shut up, our Andy.' But Andy wouldn't.

'We saw him when we were here last night.'

Andy shouldn't have said that. The man grabbed him and shook him. 'You were here last night, were you?'

'Hey, you leave my brother alone.'

The man took one look at Sandra, and let go.

'All right. Now listen. Get out of here. And stay out. Understand? This is Private Property.'

We trailed off up the path. I looked back. The man had gone inside and shut the door. Andy rubbed his arm. But he wasn't crying, for once.

50

'Anyway, he didn't get the paper,' he said triumphantly.

We turned. What paper? Andy smirked.

'A secret paper with a lot of little writing. I bet that's what he's looking for. I bet he's pretending to be the Demon Bike Rider to scare people off. I bet there's something in that cottage, bank notes or something.' He pulled a crumpled sheet from his pocket.

'Let's have a look,' I said.

Ranji nudged me. 'That man's coming out of the cottage.'

'Let's go up the old oak tree.'

'Good idea.' We set off at a run, and a couple of minutes later we were all in our places on the old tree trunk. Andy passed round the paper. His sister smoothed it out. She looked puzzled. Finally she said, 'Oh it's just some old council notice,' and passed it to me.

' "Notice is hereby given" – "hereby" they do write funny don't they. It says "Web Cottage". Never heard of that.'

'Perhaps that's the real name of Barker's. It's a funny name. Does it mean spider's web?'

'Don't know.' I read on: 'It says here "demolition".'

'That means they're going to knock it down,' said Sandra.

'Clever girl.'

'That's why the ghost is upset,' said Andy. 'First they knocked those other places down and the other ghosts went and left him on his own. Now they're going to knock down his cottage and he'll have nowhere to go.'

We laughed. Andy looked pained. His sister made a face.

'Not much of a mystery, though.'

'Oh, yes there is,' said Ranji. 'If they're going to knock the cottage down, why is that mystery man so upset about people nosing round? We weren't doing any harm. And there's nothing to knock off, is there? And why keep the place locked up?'

'Hey, it wasn't locked up the other night, was it?' Sandra remembered. 'That man must have got that lock fixed this weekend.'

'He's coming,' said Ranji suddenly.

'Who, the DBR?'

'No, you nit. The mystery man.' We looked down. The man was walking along the path towards the oak.

'Keep still. He can't see us up here.'

The man passed underneath. He was walking steadily, head down as if he were thinking about something.

He reached the top of the slope and turned down to go into the park.

'Tell you what. Let's follow him.'

'What for, Ranji?'

'Could be fun. He's stopped us going in that cottage. He's up to something. Let's follow him and find out.'

'We can't all traipse behind him through the park.'

'I know. We can run round the side, through the trees, and wait near the gate. When he gets into the street, it'll be easier.'

We dropped to the grass and ran down the slope and through the trees. When we reached the park gate the mystery man was nowhere in sight.

'Tell you something about that man,' I said. 'He's not local. He's from somewhere else.'

'I'm not so sure,' said Sandra. 'I think he was local once. He's trying to cover up the way he talks by speaking a bit posh. I bet he lived here once, went away, and now he's come back.'

'Told you,' Andy said. 'He's a bank robber and he's hidden his loot in the cottage. He's been in prison and now he wants it back and he can't find it.'

'Shut up, Andy. Perhaps he's a relative of Barker's.'

'We could ask Mr Walker. He'd know. He knows everybody in Bugletown.'

'Good idea. He may be over the other side now. Let's go and ask him.'

'We can't do that. We'll miss Mr Mystery.'

'Let's split up again, then. Sandra and Andy go and see Mr Walker, Ranji and me follow the man.'

'Don't think much of that.'

'Let's spin for it.'

By the time we'd done that the mystery man was in sight, walking down the main park road. Sandra and Ranji slipped off through the bushes to go and see Mr Walker. Andy and I waited till the mystery man had turned down Bishop's Road, then sneaked after him. We had to follow him all the way down to Station Road. It wasn't all that hard because he had his head down and never looked round once. But we kept fifty yards behind him all the time, just to be sure. At the main road, he turned right and we got to the corner just in time to see him go into the Three Fiddlers.

'Oh, Norah,' I said. 'We can't go in there after him.'

But we were in luck. The man came out a couple of minutes later with a glass of beer and sat down at a table in front of the pub. We stood at the corner of the pub yard just out of sight and waited. It was hot and I began to be thirsty. So did Andy.

'I wish I had a limeade,' he grumbled.

'Well, you can't,' I snapped. I knew now what his sister had to put up with.

'Hey, he's talking to somebody.' Andy pointed.

The mystery man was talking to another man at the table. It was Mr Whitehurst.

'Might have known he'd be in it as well,' I said. 'Didn't I tell you? Wonder what they're saying?'

'Let's get closer.' Andy started round the corner. I grabbed him just in time. Just at that moment Mr Whitehurst and the mystery man got up from the table and walked over to the road. They came just a yard or two from us. We turned round quickly and pretended to be looking through a hole in the fence. But they didn't notice us. They went past, close enough for me to hear them talking.

'As long as nothing turns up before the 31st, I see no problem,' said Whitehurst. 'Your claim's as good as any and once the place is down it'll be even better.'

A second later, they'd climbed into a car and driven off.

Andy and I looked at one another.

'I wonder what that meant?' said Andy.

'Don't know. July 31st. Let's get back up to the park and tell the others.'

We turned to go. I bumped into someone who grabbed my arm.

'What do you think you're doing here?'

8

'Who, Me? Yes, You.'

I looked up. The voice was familiar. It was Sis with a young man.

'What are you doing? Lunching at the Three Fiddlers? You should be home,' she said.

'Oh, we were just looking round,' I said casually.

Not Andy though. 'We were following Mr Whitehurst and a mystery man,' he squeaked, 'and I've got a mystery paper and there's a ghost up at Barker's Bonk.'

'Oh, shut up, Andy,' I said. 'I mean, you can't take him anywhere.'

Sis and the bloke smiled. It's weird the appeal that kid has for unsuspecting adults.

'You look hot, Andy. Would you like a lime-ade?'

He nodded. We sat down at the table where

Whitehurst and the mystery man had been, while Sis and the young man went into the pub. They came out five minutes later with lager and sandwiches and two limeades for us. This is the life, I thought.

'What were you saying?' Sis asked. 'It sounded really fantastic.'

Andy pulled out his piece of paper. Sis looked at it and passed it to her friend.

'Oh yes,' she said. 'You're quite right. Mr Whitehurst is up to something, though I don't know who the other man is. Have you any idea, Jim?'

The young man shrugged. 'Could be another agent. More likely the owner of the place. It's been empty for years, hasn't it, since Barker died. If Whitehurst is going ahead, he has to have an owner to sell it as well as a buyer.'

'What is he up to?' I asked. Jim took a drink of his lager.

'Mr Whitehurst, I think, plans to pull down the cottage and have the land cleared. Then I think they're going to build a golf club or something for the managers up at the refinery in Penfold.'

We stared.

'Does that mean they'll stop us playing on the Bonk?'

'Unless you play golf,' said Sis.

'That's not funny, our Sis.'

'Sorry, Mike.' She grinned. She didn't look very sorry.

'What did Mr Whitehurst mean, Sis? He was talking about it being all right by the 31st.'

'Oh, that's what the notice is about. It's to let people know that he's got permission to pull the old cottage down and clear the land unless someone's got a good reason why he shouldn't.'

'Well, we have.'

'I don't know if the council would see it that way, Mike.'

'Well, they ought.'

Jim smiled. 'I think you're right, Mike. What sort of place is this – Web Cottage. Is it very old?'

Sis shrugged. 'I don't know, Jim. Old Barker died ages ago, before I was born.'

'There used to be three cottages up there,' I said.

'How do you know, Mike?'

I told them about the foundations we'd discovered in the grass.

'That's funny,' said Sis. 'I thought there was only one place up there. I'll get Mr Hollis to look it up. Could be interesting.'

I remembered something else.

'What did old Whitehurst mean when he said, "your claim is as good as any"?'

Jim frowned: 'Are you sure you heard right, Mike? That sounds peculiar. Unless this other man reckons to be some relation of Barker.'

'Sandra and Ranji are asking Mr Walker about that right now,' I said.

'Got everything covered, haven't you? I hope your brother doesn't make up his mind to investigate me, Laura.'

She grinned at him. 'Why, have you got something to hide?'

I could see that they were getting more interested in each other than in our mystery. So I nudged Andy. We got up to go.

'We'll be off to find the others. Thanks for the drink, Sis.'

We walked off out of the yard. Sis was so busy listening to Jim, she never even noticed us going.

Andy and I trailed back up the hill. It was hotter than ever now and the streets were dusty. The others were lying under the trees when we got there, eating ice cream.

'Where've you been?' they demanded.

We ignored the question and sat down. We told them all we'd found out and they listened without saying a word.

'What did you find out from Mr Walker?' I asked.

'Not much. He seemed bothered about something. Hey, wait a minute, though. He did say that old Barker had no relations. That's why the cottage has been empty for so long. There's been no one to sell it.'

'Then who's that bloke who kicked us out?'

'Who knows? And – why did Whitehurst say – "your claim's as good as anybody's"?' Sandra sat up.

'You know, something really weird's going on up at Barker's Bonk.'

'You reckon?' I said in mock surprise.

'Don't be sarky, Mike,' Sandra retorted. 'Listen.' She began to count off on her fingers:

'First, people start seeing the Demon Bike Rider, whoever, or whatever that is. He digs for something in that old garden. Then he hides his tools in the oak. That's strange. Next, the mystery man turns up at the cottage and gets stroppy with us. Then, the mystery man is up to something with old Whitehurst.'

We all looked at her.

'I think it's all part of the same thing,' she added.

'How?' asked Ranji.

'Mystery man and DBR are the same thing.

He's after something in the old house and he's trying to scare other people away.'

'You're wrong, Sandra,' I interrupted. 'Why did the mystery man tell us off for digging in the garden, if he's the DBR and he's been doing the digging himself?'

'He's trying to fool us,' said Ranji. 'No, there's something funny. Why should they suddenly lock that door? It's been open for donkey's years.'

'I say we find out,' put in Sandra.

'How?' I was suspicious.

'Get in there again. The top window's open. We could climb in.'

'Mystery man might spot us again.'

She shook her head: 'Not if we go in there at night.'

I jumped up. 'Oh no, Sandra. Not after what happened the other night. We could really be caught.'

She shrugged: 'So what can mystery man do if he catches us?'

'I don't know about mystery man. It's the Demon Bike Rider I'm thinking about.'

'But, it's the same bloke, I'm telling you.' Sandra was getting angry.

So was I.

'You don't know. Suppose it isn't!'

Andrew piped up: 'Well, I don't really want to go back into that old dump.'

No one spoke for a while. Then Sandra gave a cunning smile.

'All right, Mike. Let's try another way. Let's investigate it at Whitehurst's end.'

'How?' I asked.

'I'm not sure *how*. But I know *who* can.'

'Who?'

'You, Mike!'

9

Mike Baxter, Private Eye

I stared at Sandra.

'You're off your trolley. It must be the heat. What do I do? Burgle Whitehurst's safe?'

'Well, not exactly. But you could go to his office when your mum goes there to clean. And see if you can sort of spot anything.'

I pulled a face. 'Look, Sandra. Anything for a joke. But that's risky.'

'It's not a joke. Listen, Mike. If no one objects by July 31st, old Whitehurst gets to pull down that old cottage and clears the Bonk. And we won't be able to come up here any more. Right?'

'Right.'

'So if we can find something that proves the mystery man has no right to sell the cottage, that's a good reason for stopping Whitehurst, isn't it?'

I couldn't argue round that one.

'But what do I tell Mum?'

'Tell her you'd like to help with the work.'

I gawped.

'Me?'

'Yes. You. Say you're bored. Say you want a new experience in life – like work.'

'Ha, ha.'

'Look, Mike. Is it worth a try, or isn't it? If we find anything out and save Barker's Bonk you'll be a hero.'

I snorted. But when I thought about it I rather liked the idea. Not being a hero, I mean, but doing the private eye bit. Who knows, maybe I had a talent that way.

'OK. But suppose I don't find anything?'

She shrugged. 'Let's cross that bridge when we get there.'

I nodded. 'OK. But I'm getting hungry. I only had a light lunch at the Three Fiddlers,' I said casually. 'I'm off home. See you.'

'Mike, we forgot,' said Ranji. 'Mr Walker's letting us have some young trees to plant. Says they need a new home, urgently. We're going out tonight to plant them.'

'Where?'

'Oh, don't know. Like Bill says, drop one in here, one in there.'

I shook my head.

'Can't come with you, sorry. Mum says I've been out late too much this week. I'll have to stay in. Besides, if I'm going to do a Frank Cannon in Whitehurst's office tomorrow I need to get to bed early. Mum's up at half past six.'

'OK,' they said. 'Meet you afterwards – at the oak.'

I was putting it on a bit. But I had to be up at seven to go out with Mum next morning when she set off on her cleaning round. I asked if I could come along and help her empty wastepaper baskets and do odd jobs. She looked at me strangely.

'You feeling all right, son?'

'Oh quite. I thought it would be fun to give you a hand for once.'

'Fun is not the word I would use, Mike. Still if you insist, get a move on, lad.'

By eight o'clock we were in Whitehurst's flash office in Station Road. I helped Mum tidy up and watched while she Hoovered the carpet. Then when she had finished his room and was busy in the main office, I sneaked back into his office. I could hardly believe my eyes.

There, right in the middle of the polished top of

the desk was a brown folder. And it had a label: 'Web Cottage, development'. I listened. The vacuum cleaner was still going. I opened the folder. There was a stack of papers, letters, a map, and – what was that?

I slid the paper half out of the folder. It was a sketch plan of the Bonk – it even had the old cottage foundations marked in with dotted lines. And there was the old oak – with a BIG BLACK CROSS right over it. Old Whitehurst was going to cut down our oak as well. He wasn't satisfied with knocking down the cottage. He was chopping our oak. I looked a bit further. My hands were shaking. The letters had different names on them, but one was there several times. Arthur Hayes, with an address in Australia. Could that be the mystery man? But Australia?

The door slammed. I jumped like a rabbit, stuffed the papers back, shut the folder and raced back into the general office. I was busy with a duster, when in, like a whirlwind, rushed Mr Whitehurst.

'Good morning, Mr Whitehurst, you are early,' said Mum.

He didn't say a word. He charged straight through into his own room and picked up the phone.

'What's got into him this bright, sunny morning?'

muttered Mum as she ran a damp cloth along the window ledge.

We soon found out.

'Police,' bellowed Mr Whitehurst. 'Inspector Parkinson . . . Oh, I see, well Sergeant . . . oh, it's you Constable Hadley. Now listen carefully, Constable. I want a plain-clothes man sent up to my house in Bishop's Road immediately. Yes, a plain-clothes man. I don't want the neighbours to think – oh, never mind. My garden has been invaded by vandals. What's that? What have they done? They have been planting trees, Constable. Trees in my garden. What do you mean, there's no law against it?'

Through the half-open door I could see Mr Whitehurst jump up and walk round the desk at the end of the telephone wire, like a dog on a lead.

'No, the trees did *not* seed themselves, Constable. How do I know? Because two of them were planted upside down!'

He slammed the door shut with his foot. But I'd heard enough. Some genius had done a 'pop one in here' act with Mr Walker's young trees in Whitehurst's garden. I giggled. Serve him right though. He was going to chop *our* tree down.

The outer door opened. I looked up. Oh no. There, six feet away from me, was the mystery man.

I caught his eye for a second and then I bent down over a wastepaper basket and pretended to be polishing it. He stopped a second and then walked past me and knocked on Whitehurst's office door.

'Mum,' I said. 'I've just remembered something urgent.'

She laughed. 'Had enough already, Mike? You'll not last out to draw your pension, that's for sure. All right – off you go. I'll be home at dinner time. We'll have spaghetti.'

'Oh, smashing, Mum. Tinned?'

'Get off with you – what d'you take me for?'

As I was leaving, Mr Whitehurst's door opened and he called:

'Mrs Baxter!'

He seemed even more stroppy now. I didn't wait for more details, but shot off up Station Road and didn't stop until I was in the park. I was puffed out when I reached the oak. The branches opened and Ranji's face poked through.

'Here comes Baxter, the fifty-minute mile man.'

I made a rude noise and climbed up the slope. Once I was in the tree I let the others wait for a minute before I told the tale. I was out of breath anyway, and it did them good to wait.

'All right, Mike,' said Sandra. 'Don't keep us in suspenders. What's happened?'

'Old Whitehurst's going to cut down this old tree, that's what . . .' I told them what I'd seen in the folder on his office desk. They looked dumbstruck. But I hadn't finished with them yet.

'Which nit stuck trees in Whitehurst's garden?' Sandra stared. 'That must have been Andy.'

Andy looked sheepish.

'He sneaked off while Ranji and I were busy planting trees on that waste ground near Bishop's Road.'

Andy shrugged: 'That waste ground was too hard and dry for planting anything.'

'Anyway, Whitehurst found out. You planted two trees upside down. And he's called the police.' I rubbed it in. Andy looked miserable.

Sandra turned up her nose: 'I can't see Constable Hadley getting his handcuffs in a twist over tree-planting, can you?'

I shook my head. I couldn't see Constable Hadley getting excited about anything short of an earthquake. 'There's something else, though. The mystery man was in Whitehurst's office.'

'Did he spot you?'

'Don't know. Hope not.'

'I think Mike did well,' said Ranji.

The other two nodded.

'That's right,' said Sandra. 'And after what he's

found out, we've got to do something – quickly.'

'Quickly?'

'Yes. July 31st is in a week's time. If we don't do something smart, the old oak will be done for. And that's even more important than Barker's old dump. We've got to have one more go to find out what the mystery man is looking for up there. That's the key to it all.'

She stopped and looked in a friendly way at me – too friendly, I thought.

'So, Mike. I'm afraid there's only one way.'

'Oh, no,' I said.

'Oh yes, Mike. We've got to go back to old Barker's place, after dark when no one will spot us.'

I protested loudly. 'You seem to have forgotten about the Demon Bike Rider!'

'Come on, Mike,' said Ranji. 'I am just as frightened as you are, but what else can we do?'

He was right, I knew. I looked at Andrew. He wasn't saying anything. Even if he was scared, he'd follow his sister anywhere.

'Good for you, Mike,' said Sandra. 'Now, we'll need a torch. Can you bring one?'

I nodded.

Ranji said: 'I'll bring a ladder. We use it for cleaning bedroom windows. It'll just reach.'

'Right. We'll meet here, half past nine. Don't be late.'

We charged off through the park. As we said chccrio, Ranji shouted:

'Hey! It's going to be fun.'

He was right. But my fun started before the others' did.

10

Enter Everybody

Mum and Dad were both home when I got there. Dad must have been on early turn and he was still in his boiler suit. He was looking grim.

But it was Mum who started the bowling.

'Michael Baxter. What have you been up to?'

I tried to block that one. 'What do you mean, Mum?'

'You know very well. Old Whitehurst called me in after you went and said someone had been messing about with his papers. And you were the only one in that office after I went out. I said I was sorry, you must have knocked the folder when you were dusting.'

I started to nod, hopefully, but Mum went on.

'Then the other bloke who was there said he'd seen you messing about up at Barker's cottage.

And on top of that, Whitehurst thinks you've got something to do with this daft business with his garden.'

'But Mum . . .'

'I've not done yet. He says he'll regard the papers as an accident. But whatever you think you're up to, it has to stop, and if there's any more trouble, I'll lose my job.'

'Oh, Mum . . . but . . .'

'Mike,' said Dad, 'I think you should tell us just what you have been up to. All of it.'

I had no choice. While I was telling the story, Sis came in: it was half-day closing at the library. She filled in some of the bits about the demolition notice. That made it seem a little less daft. But I left out the bit about our plans for going up to the cottage that evening.

'Well,' said Dad, when I'd finished. 'Perhaps this man hasn't got such a good claim to own the cottage. That's why he's so touchy. But I can't see old Whitehurst up to that kind of fiddle. I know he fancies himself, but I thought he was above board.'

'Hm,' said Mum. 'There are more ways of killing the cat . . .'

'No, I expect that if there *is* a fiddle, it's this other bloke. But there's an acre or two of land there. And if his big deal comes off, old Whitehurst'll make a quid or two. But it's a pity nothing can be done to stop him knocking that old place down. Golf club? The refinery people have got their own club in Penfold. Some people get away with murder,' said Dad.

Mum, Dad and our Sis were so busy talking they didn't seem to notice me any more. I walked into the kitchen and turned the telly on. I heard Dad say to Mum:

'Hey, Betty love. What did you say to old Whitehurst when he told you you'd lose your job?'

'Well, Tom. I told him he could . . .'

'Our Mum!' shrieked Sis.

'I told him he could Hoover his own carpets,' finished Mum.

Later that evening I slipped out. Mum and Dad thought I was upstairs reading. I didn't say anything because too many questions could have been awkward. With my torch in my pocket I sneaked off up the road, over the park and up to the old tree. The weather was still warm, but the sky wasn't clear any more. Big purple clouds had filled the sky. The air was heavy, just like before a thunderstorm. But that was just as well, because it was dark more quickly. There was no one about on the Bonk except

our gang. Sandra and Ranji were there carrying the ladder. Andy had a small hammer.

'What's that for?' I asked.

'Oh, he got some idea of tapping the walls to see if they're hollow,' said Sandra. 'Come on.'

The sun had disappeared altogether when we got to the cottage, and there was just a line of white on the horizon. The rest was dark. We put the ladder up against the cottage window. Ranji went first, then Andy, then Sandra, then me.

'Shall I pull the ladder up?' Ranji asked.

'No,' I said. 'We might need that in a hurry. Now, I reckon Andrew should keep watch by the window, while we three search this top room.'

'Why me?' said Andrew, pushing his lower lip out.

'Oh, Mike,' Sandra urged, 'let's get on with it. We'll all keep our eyes open. I know the DBR's scarey, but you can see him coming a mile off.'

'And hear him,' added Ranji. He sang:

'*Hitinkati shan efasee . . .*'

'Get moving you idiots, and shut up,' hissed Sandra.

I switched on the torch. I stood it on the window ledge while we searched the top room. There was nothing: a couple of loose boards but only dirt and an old mouse nest underneath.

'Downstairs now.'

We went through it all again in the two down-stairs rooms. But we found nothing.

'We'll have to try the garden,' said Sandra.

'Oh, no,' I said. 'We can't search that dump. Besides, my battery's going to run out soon.'

'Listen,' squeaked Andy. He tapped with his hammer on the chimney bricks. 'One's loose.'

'Let's see.'

'I can do it.'

'No you can't.'

Andy and his sister scuffled. The brick fell out and hit the floor with a thump. Something else fell with it.

'It's an old tin.'

It was an old tea tin. There was a woman's face on the side, covered with dust – Queen Victoria, I guess.

'Let's open it.'

'No, let's get back to the old oak.'

'No, let's have a look now. Put it on the floor.'

We were so excited that we forgot all about keeping watch. We all crouched down on the cottage floor round the tin in the light of my torch.

'It won't open.'

'Give it to me. You're too weak.'

'All right, Samson. See if you can do better.'

77

I'd just passed the tin to Ranji, when I heard something that made my heart jump. It was a scratching sound at the door behind us.

Someone was opening it.

We were all on our feet in a flash.

'What shall we do?' squealed Andrew.

'Upstairs, quick,' said Sandra.

We reached the top room as the front door went open with a crash. Sandra was out of the window and down the ladder with Andy after her, grunting as he banged his knee on the window frame. Somebody was tramping up the stairs as Ranji climbed out. There was a tearing noise and some foul language. Somebody had put his size elevens through the rotten old staircase.

I started to climb out when I saw the ladder had slipped. I tried to turn round to drop down when someone grabbed me. Mr Whitehurst was glaring down at me. With a wriggle I pulled free and dropped, falling over and giving my head a bang that made it ring like an alarm clock.

As I picked myself up, the cottage door flew open again. I ran for it. The others were by the gate. It was daft, but was I glad they'd waited.

'Run!' I yelled.

We ran. There were two men after us. One was Mr Whitehurst, the other must have been the

mystery man. We ran fast, but the mystery man
was running faster, and as we got near the oak he
was only twenty yards behind. In the shadows I
could see something black. It looked like a parked
car. The mystery man was almost on us, when
Ranji shouted to Andy:

'Throw the box to me.'

Ranji caught the box and leapt for the tree. But
he didn't climb into it. He dived feet first into the
hole at the roots and vanished. He'd gone clean
through and slid down the slope beneath. Before
he could stop himself the mystery man had followed
him. But the hole wasn't his size. With a grunt
he stuck fast. I could have laughed. I *would*
have laughed, but Mr Whitehurst's hand was
on my collar, half choking me. He reached out
another hand and grabbed Andy. That was a bad
move.

Next moment Sandra dived on Mr Whitehurst,
punching like mad. He let go of Andy. I jerked
myself free just as the mystery man heaved himself
up from the tree hole. I was a prisoner again. I
could tell when mystery man's fingers gripped my
arm that I wasn't going to get free from him. He
reached out his other arm and pulled Sandra off
Mr Whitehurst.

'Now,' grunted Mr Whitehurst. 'We'll get these

hooligans to the car and take them straight down to the police station.'

'Police station?' I demanded.

'Yes. Police station, young man. I think there'll be a matter of trespass and possibly theft. Come on.'

Mystery man jerked me by my collar. All five of us started towards the car.

But we never reached it. Mr Whitehurst was in the lead, holding Andrew by the arm, when he stopped suddenly and we nearly crashed into him.

'What's that?'

He pointed to the moors. In the black distance a yellow wavering light appeared. It drew closer and closer.

'I don't know,' said mystery man.

But we knew. Andrew started to whimper and Sandra put out her free hand to comfort him.

Behind the light the weird black figure took shape. And then came the weirder chanting noise:

> *'Hitinkati shan efasee . . .*
> *Ha pohem lof liazadree . . .'*

I saw the amazed faces of Mr Whitehurst and the mystery man. I was right. They knew even less about this than we did.

The Demon Bike Rider was riding and this time we couldn't escape. We were right in his path.

11

DBR's Last Ride

In the split second we heard the dirge, everyone stood still. Then the eerie figure was almost on us and Sandra took her chance. She jerked loose.

'Come on, Mike, Andy. Run for it.'

She shot off. I jerked my arm. Mystery man, caught off balance, let go and jumped after her. They ran right in the path of the ghost.

The light suddenly shot down as if the Rider's cycle had fallen. A black shape moved between Sandra and the mystery man. She screamed. There came a crunching sound. The mystery man groaned and dropped to the grass.

Mr Whitehurst let go of Andrew, jumped to the door of his car and switched on his headlights. In the next instant everything showed up in the blaze of light.

There was Mr Whitehurst jumping back from his car. A few yards away the mystery man, holding his head, struggled to his feet. Beyond him was Sandra, her eyes wide and wild.

And, in the middle, fists up like Mohammed Ali, was . . .

'MR WALKER!' we three shouted.

Mr Walker, the Demon Bike Rider.

Everybody began to talk at once – or rather shout. It went on for ten minutes, getting louder and more mixed up. Then suddenly it stopped as Dad arrived with a torch looking for me. They'd found out at home that I wasn't upstairs reading.

Dad suggested everyone came down to our house, and before very long we were all sitting round the kitchen table and Mum had the big teapot out.

The mystery man – his name was Arthur Hayes – was very quiet. He kept rubbing the blue bump where the DBR, I mean Mr Walker, had hit him. Mr Whitehurst wasn't quiet, though. He started to talk about a lot of things, breaking and entering and theft and various other charges. He'd spotted our light in the cottage. You can see Barker's cottage from Bishop's Road. Finding us up there just wrapped it all up for him.

Dad put on what Sis calls his 'Mr Chairman' voice.

'First of all, Mr Whitehurst, how can you break and enter a place that's been a dump for twenty-odd years?'

'Nearer thirty,' said Mr Walker.

'Second,' Dad went on, 'are you making the charge as the owner? Because if you are the owner I'm going to complain to the Council about it. It's scandalous the way that cottage has gone to rack and ruin.'

'I'm not the owner,' snapped Mr Whitehurst. 'Mr Hayes is the owner. I'm arranging the sale of the property for him.'

'How are you the owner?' said Mr Walker staring at Hayes. 'Old Barker didn't leave it to anybody. That's why it's been empty.'

'I'm his next of kin,' replied Arthur Hayes. 'His nephew-in-law or something like that.'

'You, never!' snorted Mr Walker. 'Hey, wait a minute! You're Minnie Hayes' son.'

Arthur Hayes nodded. 'Right. When Mum died, I emigrated. Barker had a cousin who went out to Australia about forty years ago. We met up – both from the same town – and I married his daughter. We only found out about Barker's place this year – from an old letter.'

'All right,' said Dad, taking charge again. 'What about theft? What's been stolen?'

Mr Whitehurst coughed.

'We have reason to believe there is a document, which may or may not be the late Mr Barker's will.'

'Aha,' said Mr Walker. 'Now I see. You're afraid Old Barker might have left it to the Cat's Home. He might, too, the mean old devil.'

'There's only an old tin box,' I said. 'And Ranji's got that.'

'Right,' said Dad. 'Our Sis can go round to Ranji's and ask his parents if he can kindly bring it round here. In the meantime I suggest we have a cup of tea and calm down.'

Our Sis got her coat on and went out. Sandra turned to Mr Walker.

'So you're the Demon Bike Rider after all?'

'Demon Who?'

'We saw this weird figure,' explained Sandra, 'with horns, and a yellow light – and it was howling. And we followed it to Barker's Cottage. It was digging. And there were tools left under the old oak.'

For a second or two Mr Walker looked blank. Then he smiled, then he chuckled, then he began to laugh until he choked on his tea. It was catching.

Mum and Dad joined in. Even Arthur Hayes started. Only Mr Whitehurst wasn't amused.

'I see now,' gasped Mr Walker. 'I was carrying young trees on my back, to plant them in old Barker's garden. It seemed fair enough. After all he'd chopped so many down, and he didn't need the land any more. Then,' he nodded at Mr Whitehurst, 'when I heard the land was going to be cleared, I thought I'd have to shift some of the small ones I'd just planted. I left some of the gear under the tree one night when I had too much to carry.'

'Oh, so that was where the trees came from – the ones you gave us, and Andy planted . . .' Sandra stopped and looked at Mr Whitehurst. But he was brooding over something and took no notice.

'What was that noise you were making, Mr Walker?' I asked. 'It was weird.'

'What noise?'

I tried to imitate it.

He stared at me, then he began to laugh again.

'Believe it or not, that is a song. It's called "Trees", a very fine song. I've got an old record of Richard Tauber singing it.

> *"I think that I shall never see*
> *A poem lovely as a tree."* '

'That explains everything,' said Sandra, Andy and I together.

Just then, Sis arrived with Ranji, holding the tin and looking worried. He held it out.

'I haven't opened it, Mr Whitehurst.'

'Just as well,' said Dad. He turned to Arthur Hayes. 'Well, Mr Hayes. I suppose this is yours. Or I reckon *you* should open it.'

Arthur Hayes looked nervous. He struggled with the lid. But it was jammed tight. Dad got an old screwdriver and prised the box open. Inside were four pieces of paper, brown and stained. They looked very old. They were all handwritten, funny old writing with squiggles and whirls.

Arthur Hayes looked them over, carefully. 'I can't read them properly. They're very old. Perhaps hundreds of years old.' He was looking happier now. 'One thing's sure. It's not a will of Mr Barker's.'

'Which means,' said Mr Whitehurst, looking smug, 'that Mr Hayes is without doubt the owner, as the next of kin.' He looked meaningfully at Dad. 'But, in view of everything, I think we'll forget about breaking and entering, etc.'

'That's nice,' said Mr Walker, 'then perhaps Sandra and Mike and Andrew will forget about charges of assault.'

'Not sure if *I* will,' said Arthur Hayes. But he was grinning. He got up to go with Mr Whitehurst and thanked Mum for the cup of tea. He didn't seem such a bad bloke after all.

When they'd gone, Mum said, 'They forgot the papers.'

'They didn't seem all that interested in them,' said Dad.

'Tell you what,' said Sis. 'I don't suppose they'd mind if I took them into the library. Mr Hollis, who looks after the old town records, will be very interested.'

'Well, then,' said Mum. 'I think you children had better be making tracks for bed.'

'I'll see them home,' said Dad, getting his jacket on.

'Can I come?' I asked.

'No, my lad, you can't. You've stirred it up enough today,' said Mum.

12

Mrs Whitehurst
Makes a Suggestion

Mum's not daft, you know. She could tell that, one way or another, we were all feeling a bit down, the way things had turned out over Barker's Bonk. So she said I could invite Sandra, Andy and Ranji round to tea the next day. She did us a smashing spread and it cheered us up. The thunderstorm that was building up the night before had blown away, and the sky was clear again. We could see the top of the Bonk from the kitchen window.

'Well, we'll have to make the most of it until the 31st,' said Sandra.

'Well,' said Mum. 'I don't suppose it'll be cleared all at once. It'll probably be a few weeks. Till you go back to school. Then, by the half-term, who knows what'll happen.'

We sat and thought about that, to see if the thought helped.

Just then, the front door slammed and Sis came in.

'You're home early, love,' said Mum.

'Mr Hollis said I could take time off to come and tell you.'

'Tell me what?' said Mum.

'Not you, Mum, the kids.'

'Hey, what?' we all asked at once.

'Those old papers in the tin. I took them in to Mr Hollis. He hasn't had a full look at them yet, because they're so creased they'll have to be specially treated before we can open them up – they're so old. But he's seen enough . . .'

'Enough for what, Sis?'

'Web Cottage, that's Barker's Cottage and the other two, are at least 500 years old.'

'Never!'

'It's true. They're weavers' cottages, built when Elizabeth I was a girl.'

'Weavers' cottages?'

'Yes. The weavers used to live and work there. They each had a loom in the upstairs room. They worked terrifically hard, long hours . . .'

'That's nothing,' grinned Ranji. 'My dad works dozens of looms at a time.'

'I know, Ranji. But this was before they brought modern machines in. That's why Web Cottage is so important.'

'How?' I asked.

'Oh, don't be so slow, Mike. Barker's old cottage is important as history. Mr Hollis went to see the Chief Librarian this afternoon. And it looks as though they can get the Council to put a preservation order on the cottage.'

'What does that do?'

'Well, I'll tell you what it does. It stops old Whitehurst from pulling it down, for a start. Whatever big plans he has on the Bonk, if it's going to be sold, the cottage will have to be kept. Mr Hollis reckons the Council may take the lot over, rebuild the other houses and make it look as it used to be for people to come and see. And the old papers you found will go in the Museum. Well, aren't you pleased?'

'Yes,' said Sandra, slowly. 'But what about the tree?'

'What tree?'

'The old oak.'

'Oh, you mean that one that's practically falling down. I don't know. I mean, what's that got to do with it?' said Sis.

'If you can't see that,' I said, 'then it's no use our explaining.'

Sis shrugged. 'Sorry. Anyway, I've got to rush back. I thought you'd like to know. When we know all the details, there might be a story in the local paper about it.'

'Big deal,' I muttered. But Sis had gone.

After we'd finished tea, we drifted up to the Bonk and climbed the oak again.

'It's a funny thing,' said Sandra, stroking the tree's rough old bark. 'People can't see that trees are as important as old buildings. Even if they haven't got papers to prove it.'

'Mr Walker understands,' said Ranji.

'Oh, I know. But how long would you have to wait before one of his new trees grew as big as this one, I bet this tree's as old as that cottage.'

'Get off,' I said. 'Five hundred years? Don't be daft.'

'She's probably right, you know.'

Who said that? We stared at one another, then we looked down. There was Mrs Whitehurst, standing on the path. She had only one dog with her today.

'Oh Mrs Whitehurst, you gave us a shock,' said Sandra.

'Not as much of a shock as Ranji gave me, with his rope trick,' she answered.

'I know,' said Sandra. 'We really ought to say

sorry to you about that, and about those trees our Andy stuck in your garden.'

Mrs Whitehurst smiled. 'Oh those. Don't apologize. Now they're the right way up, they'll look very well.'

'But,' I said, 'Mr Whitehurst was furious about the trees. He rang the police.'

'I know. But I think he's changed his mind. At least I think I've got him to change his mind.'

'Thank you, Mrs Whitehurst,' said Ranji. 'But I'm afraid Mr Whitehurst won't be pleased about it if the Council takes Barker's Cottage and doesn't let him build a golf club.'

Mrs Whitehurst smiled.

'News travels fast, doesn't it? You heard already. Oh I think Mr Whitehurst will be a little disappointed, but not too much. The Council will pay for the cottage, though not as much as selling the land for a golf club would make.'

'That's all right for Mr Hayes and Mr Whitehurst,' I said, 'but what about our old tree?'

'Your old tree?' She looked puzzled.

'Our Sis – my sister – says they'll only bother about keeping the cottage. So the old oak may get chopped down.'

'Oh, that's bad,' she said.

It was, too. We couldn't think of anything else to say, and everyone was quiet for a bit.

Then suddenly Mrs Whitehurst smiled as if she'd had a pleasant thought.

'Of course, there is something you could do.'

'Oh, what's that, Mrs Whitehurst?'

'You could get a preservation order on the tree.'

'Preservation order? I thought that was only for old houses,' said Sandra.

'Old trees are history, too,' replied Mrs White-hurst, 'and I'm willing to bet this old tree has seen more history even than that old cottage. If I were you, I'd go right down to the library and find out.'

We didn't need telling twice.

When I got back home to tell Mum, Dad was home from work just finishing his tea. He looked out of the window.

'You know, Betty. That little bit of rain we had the other night didn't help the garden much. I'll just have to get that hose mended.'

'Tom Baxter,' said Mum. 'If I were you I'd leave that hose alone. It's such an old relic now they're bound to put a preservation order on it.'

CHALLENGE IN THE DARK

Robert Leeson

Mike Baxter's first day at his new school marks the start of an unforgettable and challenging week – not least when he makes an enemy of Steven Taylor and his bullying older brother, Spotty Sam. Mike's friends 'help out' by setting up a dare for both him and his enemy Steven Taylor – to stay in an old disused underground shelter. Before either has much time to protest they find themselves exposed to real dangers, experiencing fear and panic as a result of more than playground victimization.

'This short adventure has the same unmistakable veracity and friendly humour that has made *The Demon Bike Rider* so popular with young readers.' *Growing Point*

The Demon Bike Rider by Robert Leeson is also in Lions.

My Best Fiend
SHEILA LAVELLE

'My best friend is called Angela Mitchell and she lives in the house next door.' There is nothing unusual about this opening description Charlie Ellis gives of her best friend, but the tales that follow reveal the very unusual scrapes these two friends seem to get into.

Pretty Angela's marvellous ideas usually lead to disaster. Like the time they got stuck on a single-track railway bridge over the River Thames with the rattle of train wheels getting closer and closer; and the time Angela accidentally caught an escaped circus lion in the back garden. But when Angela suggested burning down her dad's garage so that he could claim the insurance for a new one, Charlie really thought things had gone a bit too far. For somehow it's always plainer Charlie who ends up taking the blame, and the spelling mistake in her English essay really wasn't much of a mistake at all.